Grishm
The Summer of Life

Flairs and Glairs
Publication House

"Grishm-The Summer of Life"

ISBN No: " 978-93-90799-03-9"
1st Edition
Language – English and Hindi

Flairs and Glairs
Publication House
Regd. Under MSME Act.

Disclaimer

This is a work of fiction and solely represent the thoughts of the corresponding authors of the articles. Our editors have tried their best to edit the content of all the authors and check the plagiarism.
All the write-ups in this book are unique and are only published in this book.
In case any plagiarism or error is found, only the author is responsible alone, and not the publisher or the Compilers.

Cover Designing and Book Formatting
Shubham Shah and Ishani Agarwal

Acknowledgement

First of all, I thank God, for this life, as a human, has been a lesson full of experiences that have moulded me into the person I am today. To destiny, for teaching me lessons that no one else could.

I'd like to thank my parents for their support, without them, I'd be nothing. My sibling, Nishita Ninave, for her help, support and the blessing she is in my life.

I pay gratitude to my friends Avnish Kumar, Alolika Ray, Momo, Pavan Sharma, Ankita Kumar, and Anandhini Iyappan. You people are not just my friends but are my guiding angels who I know I can blindly rely upon.

Shubham Shah and the entire team of Flairs and Glairs, I salute your dedication and helping nature. You are the reason why the book was possible.

Last but not the least, all the co-authors who were extremely cooperative throughout the project. You all are the whole and soul of the book. All I wish is health and happiness for you all!

Co-authors

Shubham Shah (Founder, Flairs and Glairs)
Ishani Agarwal (Co-founder, Flairs and Glairs)
Grishma Ninave (Compiler)

1. Nishita Ninave
2. Shivansh Sharma
3. Abhilash Sharma
4. Sahina Ghugha
5. Jeevitha.S
6. Shivani Jha
7. Anand Jain
8. Himani Mehra
9. S. Vasha Varthini
10. Pratima Yadav" Shaani"
11. Sanskriti Basu
12. Vishali.S
13. Suma an Indian
14. Giftson Jose
15. Durga Singh Thakur
16. Mansha Poddar
17. Deepti Bagde
18. Vidhi Bhadreshbhai Desai
19. Aarya Jha
20. Yashika Karamchandani
21. Ishwari Kishor Shirur
22. Kanupriya Rastogi
23. Aishwarya Garg
24. Priya Jha
25. Lakshmi Soni
26. R.Susanna Celsia
27. Kalamkaar

28. Sarvesh Bagde
29. Rashmi Baweja
30. Arkapriya Ghosh
31. Moumita Bagchi
32. Krishna Motwani
33. Hema Kirthiga J
34. Diksha Motwani
35. Gautam Balasaheb Kardile
36. Varsha Fatakale Warade
37. Shivani Bhardwaj
38. Amir Javed
39. Priyanka Ramakant Kadam
40. Jayashree Sahoo
41. Archana Paryani
42. Deepjyoti Chowdhury
43. Yamini Sona Vaishnavi
44. Sri Harsha Vineela Balla
45. Christy Gnana Deepa. J
46. Amritanshu Shreshth
47. Shivani Batra
48. Kanchi Gupta
49. Keshav Tibrewal
50. Bhavika Dhiraj Sindhi

Shubham Shah

(Founder- Flairs and Glairs)

Shubham Shah, an entrepreneur at "Flairs & Glairs" a brand with dynamics in events organizing and cultural educational pan INDIA, is a 26yrs old guy who recently has entered the digital platform of imprinting emotions. He has initiated with his own open mic platform to help budding poets and aspiring writers under his brand named as "Teekhe Zasbaaat"

He is a commerce graduate from the Bhagalpur City of Bihar. He states Writing has impersonated him since childhood and he has now been writing for over a decade!
Cooking, on the other hand, is his passion! He also mentions, trying out new things just tickles him!
When asked sir, Why SPICY EMOTIONS?
He smiled and added, "agar jasbaat teekhe na ho toh wo jasbaat kahan" Spices are all that blends! So do his words!
As a chef, he presents to you his dish! Hot and freshly served! Taste it! Feel it! Enjoy it! You can also find his writing in the Book "Teekhe Zasbaaat" and 50+ Co-authored anthologies. With his passion to explore opportunities across Platforms, he is working with keen devotion and We wish him all the very best for his future ventures.
He is Featured in the **International Magazine De-Mode** for his upcoming solo novel.
He is **Approved by Ne8x for its Lit Fest,** and is a **Golden Star Awards 2020 Winner.**
He is an **India Book of Records Holder** for his Anthology **Satrang,** and has the **Grandmaster** title by **Asia Book of Records**, for the same.
He has also been featured in **Prabhat Khabar**, **Dainik Jagran** and other renowned Newspaper for his achievements. He has also been awarded with **India Star Republic Award 2021.**
He has been a proud co-author to
India Book of Records (Title- Black)
World Book of Records (Title -15 Wonders of Poetries)
India Book of Records (Title - Aaina)
Vajra World Records Holder (Title - Gustakhi Maaf Hai)
High Range of Records Holder (Title - Gustakhi Maaf Hai)

Share your reviews on his

INSTAGRAM

@spicy_emotions
@shubham4shah

Or via email on

shubham2shah@gmail.com

To stay tuned to his work and opportunities follow his business Handles

INSTAGRAM FACEBOOK YOUTUBE

@flairsandglairs
@teekhezasbaaat

WEBSITE:

https://flairsandglairs.in/
https://flairsandglairs.com/

Ishani Agarwal

(Co-Founder- Flairs and Glairs)

Ishani Agarwal hails from the City of Joy, Kolkata.
She is the co-founder of her Community "Teekhe Zasbaaat" and Flairs and Glairs Publication.
Been a Compiler for 45+ Anthologies, she is in the process for more. Co-authored in 150+ Anthologies. She is a India Book of Records Holder, a Vajra World Records Holder, a High Range of Records Holder and a Bravo Record holder.

Approved by Ne8x for its Lit Fest 2020, and Literary Icon 2020. Also a Golden Star Awards Winner 2020.
She has also been awarded with India Star Republic Award 2021.
She has been featured by the National Magazine "Taree Zameen Par" with the title 'unstoppable'.
Also featured in the International Magazine DeMode for her upcoming solo novel, she is proud to write on social issues, and is happy with the love she is receiving.
Connect with her on Instagram: @Ishani_agarwal_quotes / @compilations_so_far

Grishma Ninave
(Compiler)

A student of science and an admirer of arts.
A science graduate cherishing the art of writing, working as a project head at Flairs & Glairs Publication House. Published in the Editorial section of a national magazine as Aaj Ki Womaniyaa, in the first edition of 2021.
A minion millenial with extra-large dreams.
Is in active rebellion with her mother about the number of books she must have in the house.

When not reading, can be found writing and reviewing books a lot.

Firm believer that music is what can revive and reconcile the world.
She's one of those people who love greys more than colours and she's like a colourful autumn too at the same time.
Admires old school love stories and retro music.
A Capricorn girl who believes hearts are more important than physical appearances.
Is into deep talks with a very few people, but believes they are the driving force of joy in her life.
Loves traveling to places where there are mountains, trees, hills and treks.
No wonder nature's beauty strikes a chord within her.
The guiding light in her life is the quote, "Don't search for happiness, because it's not something you find, it's something you create!"

Has participated in around 150 anthologies and compiled a few titles too.

This is my dawn...

The sun is moving up,
And so am I.
Rising and shining, they say.
As the warm rays touch my body,
Energy is all I can feel.
The warmth seems to embrace me
Such that it creates
A turmoil within me
A turmoil of emotional strength,
That of vigour.
There's so much within me
Which screams with happiness,
That this is my dawn,
This is my dawn...

गरम चाय की प्याली

बस गरम चाय की प्याली हो,
और साथ प्यार करने वाली हो।
थोड़ी सी बारिश की बूंदों के बीच,
सारी दुनिया की बातें निराली हों।।

मेरी आँखों से जब वो आँखें मिलाए,
उस लम्हे में मेरी सारी दुनिया सिमट जाए।
चाय में घुली मिठास की तरह,
ज़िंदगी की परेशानियाँ घुल जाए।।

जैसे टूट के बिस्कुट चाय में गिरे,
उसकी मुस्कान में मेरा दिल डूब जाए।
चाय से निकलती भांप की तरह,
उसकी छुअन से मेरे दर्द हवा हो जाए।।

क्या बताऊँ ये जो ख़याल हैं,
दुआ कर रहा हूँ हक़ीक़त बन जाए।
मेरा उसे देखना किसी दिन,
उसकी शक़्ल पर शर्म ले आए।।

बस गरम चाय की प्याली हो,
और साथ प्यार करने वाली हो।
थोड़ी से बारिश की बूँदों के बीच,
सारी दुनिया की बातें निराली हों।।

Shivansh Sharma

He is Shivansh Sharma. Basically, from Indore but perusing MBA(Marketing &Hr) in Mysore Karnataka. He always has a passion for writing the thoughts which come into his mind. A hardcore foodie as he belongs to Indore. He is the one who is always ready to help his near ones. His life revolves around his family and friends. He is always self-motivated, enthusiastic and a person with positive vibes. He is a co-author of 20+ books and a compiler of 1 book. currently holding the position of Project Coordinator in Flairs and Glairs. His only belief is just to live happily and enjoy every moment of life. You can contact him on ig@shivanshrockzzzzz

वो दिन

जहां गया था अपनी मां को छोड़कर पहली बार ,
दोस्ती क्या होती है वो सीखा था जहां,
जहां आए भी रोते हुए थे ,
और छोड़ा भी रोते हुए था ,
वो थे हसीन लम्हे वो स्कूल के दिन,
जब भी हुए लेट तो बाहर निकाले जाते ,
हर टीचर का अजीब नाम रखते थे,
वो हर रोज़ लंच से पहले ,
टिफिन खतम का अलग मज़ा था,
हर टिफिन में अपनी हिस्सेदारी थी,
हर बार मस्ती में आगे रहते ,
बेक बेंचर का टैग शान के साथ लगाते,
क्लास रूम को क्रिकेट ग्राउंड बनाना ,
और पेंफाइट खेलना हमारा
पसंदीदा काम था ,
वो हर बार कैंटीन के समोसे खाना ,
वो बोरिंग लेक्चर कहकर बंक
पे दोस्तो के साथ जाना ,
वो अपनी टीचर पर क्रश,
वो क्लास की लड़की से पहला प्यार ,
हर वक्त उसे देखने का रश,
वो हर दीवाली पर वॉशरूम में
पटाखे फोड़ना ,
वो हर टीचर को चौकन्ना,
वो कागज के एयरोप्लेन बना कर परेशान करना ,
वो सब बड़ा याद आता है ,
वो स्कूल और स्कूल के यार बहुत याद आते है ।।।

Abhilash Sharma

Abhilash Sharma a 23 year old passionate writer. He belongs to Sonipat , Haryana . He had completed his B.com (voc) recently. He is a enthusiastic person and a sports lover as well .Worked as a co author in about 40+ anthologies inspired by Ishika Arora and Ishani Aggarwal in the field of writing .You can check out his writings on instagram at @ankahe_alfaaz_ .

ग्रीष्म :- एक फ़लसफ़ा

ज़िन्दगी की एक नायाब राह है ग्रीष्म,
गिरने के बाद फिरसे उठने की चाह है ग्रीष्म,
सर्दी के जल्द होते अंधेरे के बाद,
सूरज की वो किरणों का सवेरा है ग्रीष्म,

उम्मीदों के उस बोझ के बाद,
सफ़लता की वो राहत है ग्रीष्म,
हानियों के उन बादलों के बाद,
कुछ होते लाभों सी है वो ग्रीष्म,

सभी मायूसियों की उन वर्षाओं के बाद,
आगे बढ़ने की एक आस है वो ग्रीष्म,
हर रुकावट को पार करके,
आखरी वार करने की वो इच्छा है वो ग्रीष्म।।

Sahina Ghugha

Sahina Ghugha is a 20-year-old B.Com student at Saurashtra university Rajkot. She is from Jamnagar city of Gujarat. She is state level winner in poetry competition 2017. She is Co-author of 10+ anthologies. She is an amazing writer and poet and she wants do something for society through her pen.

Insta ID:- @Itz_Sahina_write

ग्रीष्म - एक एहसास

ये ग्रीष्म ऋत की शामें हमको
तेरी कुछ इस तरह याद दिलाती है
सूरज रंग बदल रहा है जैसे
तेरे नखरे ये शामें उठाती है।

माना की तू है बहुत ही प्यारी
पर इन शामों से भी है हमारी पक्की यारी
समेट लूं इन शामों को खुद में ऐसे
समा चुकी हो चांदनी चंदा में जैसे।

लहराती तितलियां फूलों पर यूं ही
में भंवरा और तू गुलाब हो कोई
महकती है तू भी इन शामों सी
जैसे में दीपक, और तू धूप हो कोई।

Jeevitha. S

She is a girl with stupendous writing skills. Her heart is a castle abound with unbreakable courage, being contained with enticing dreams. Penning is her way of spreading aesthetic vibes among her readers. Being a literarian is her pride. She loves to be a unicorn amidst the flock of sheep!

Him = My Happiness!

It was him who held my hands like a true gentleman, without any expectations he laid all his faith on me. He loved me with all his heart. What else would a girl need than a man like him. He not only listened to my confessions through words but he heard my heart's confessions too. It's something rare, isn't it! Yeah, it was him who heard all of me before I expressed it with grief. He wanted me to shed tears out of happiness and never out of pain. All that he did to me was something beyond a fairy-tale. He isn't my prince alone; he was my soulmate who stood as a good friend. He does rule me in a unique way that even the world couldn't, yes, he ruled my heart like a king. In this world of illusions, he was my everlasting love. I have conquered so many things and I have won many battles throughout my life until his arrival. I lost to him surrendering myself without any further delay, appointing someone to take me away as his own. And he is my love, the one for whom I was longing throughout those days. My wait is much more worthy. I agree with it now with all my whole heart ...

Shivani Jha

Shivani is in 3rd-year graduation keen to learn new things. She is passionate about writing. She has participated in many writing competitions and won them as well. She has participated in many anthologies as well. She started writing to express herself about the way women are been treated.

(1)

Contemplating the universe to replicating the human's role.
Being born and made like the planets and comets.
Pulchritudinous universe being diverse
Renaissance of us as intellectuals, I studied astrology with my spectacles.
Admiring your priceless celestial silhouette, humongously stretching arms to Longus.
Loving me like a father and nurturing me like a mother, I wanted to take your cosmopolitan further.
My parents' anger seems like an exploding sky and then enters my love to escape me from periodic high.

There is a cosmic connection, evolving without any direction.
Years passed encountering the loveless moon, I was going to enter teenage soon.
Universe's benediction of a glittery constellation, I made friends who never needed any mend.
Perfect in their own way, being mirabilis to at times being speechless.
Stuck in a pedigree of all odds I met someone like the diamond in the dust.
It seemed all beyond the skies.

Resembling the spectrum, restrained to the societal norms.
My life at that point was an epiphany of myopia transformed into presbyopia.
Everything has been dilapidated, rayless and pathless,
just like lunar and solar ellipse halting rays to illuminate within the darkness.

Universe sigh I got, sketching our love story in stellar light.
Pregrinated and regenerated thoughts to reach equinox,
I got a reason to celebrate the solstice

I didn't need any stargazer for my matrimony.
Asteroids, planets, comets attended the wedding, remarking the crimson as the colour of vermillion.
All evil eye been eradicated by vacuum pressure of the black hole.
I made my own sweet little universe.

Anand Jain

ANAND JAIN is a good writer from FAZILKA, PUNJAB
He has completed his GRADUATION in commerce stream.
From Panjab University.
He has been writing poetry for 3 years as his passion. With the help of sister (sapna jain) and brother (Rakesh jain).
He wants to be a successful banker in future.
He is a founder of ROBIN HOOD ARMY, FAZILKA (NGO).

(1)

कभी हसाती है
तो कभी सताती है
पर हर मोड़ पर वो
मेरा साथ निभाती है

कुछ दूर रह कर भी वो
कुछ यूं साथ निभाती है
कि सुनती है वो मेरा सारा पागलपन
पता नहीं वो कैसे मुझे झेल जाती है

पल में ख्फा हो जाती है
पल में मान जाती है
कह दे जो कोई मुझे बुरा भला
वो सबसे खुद ही लड़ जाती है

यूं तो बड़ी समझदार है वो
पर मेरे आगे बिल्कुल बच्ची बन जाती है
खुद करती है नादानियां
और मुझे पागल बुलाती है

हो जाती है जब वो नाराज़
तो उसकी याद बहुत सताती है
उसकी आदत हो गई है यारो मुझे
उसके बिना ये ज़िन्दगी कहां चल पाती है

(2)

ना आंखों में सुरमा लगाती है,
ना होठों पर लाली, लेकिन,
आकर्षित कर देती है मुझे अपनी तरफ
जब आंखों से ही कुछ कहते-कहते मुस्कुरा देती है !!

सादगी उसकी तो कहर ढा जाती है,
जब जाते-जाते वो अचानक मुड़ कर देख लेती है !!

पलकें उठाकर कभी नहीं देखती है मुझे,
लेकिन, बेहद मासूम लगती है,
जब अपनी भौंहें उठा कर,
होंठों को दांतों से दबा कर, कुछ सोचने लगती है !!

सादगी उसकी तो कहर ढा जाती है,
जब चेहरे पर आती हुई,
वो अपनी लटों को,
बड़े प्यार से संवारती है !!

गुलाब की तरह खिलखिलाती है वो,
जब, लाल रंग का सलवार-सूट पहनकर,
घर से निकलती है,
हवा में लहराता उसका दुपट्टा,
जैसे मुझसे कुछ कह जाता है !!

सादगी उसकी तो कहर ढा जाती है,
जब अपनी कलाई में पहने,
हर रोज़ उन चूड़ियों को वो खनकाती है ।।

Himani Mehra

Himani is in 3rd-year graduation specifically B.Tech (I.T). She is good at coding. She started writing to enhance her skills and within a month she was able to get 100 followers. She has participated in many writing competitions and won them too. She has also participated in anthologies as well.

(1)

I loved my childhood friend. we used to play, sleep, study just like best friends and I never knew how I started liking him but it was not the same at his part. For the sake of our friendship, I never told him to.

Looking at you day night, sometimes exemplifying nasty fights,
From abducting each other's belongings to having treehouse longings
Eating tubs of ice cream at night to having 4 am talks We met like shooting stars, always trying to hide magnitude scars.
Our childhood relationship if friendship, is now urging for your trustworthy companionship.
I know you don't want to portray same feelings, and won't ask for any dealings. Loving you being immortal,
and for you only our friendship is eternal. Imbibing all lessons together to gracefully hiding you from my father.
U will always be my protagonist personification. Being a concoction of grace and disgrace, you are always unique, and more than blue suits you pink.
From deteriorating my sincerity to face world's cruel reality.
From excruciating pain for me without any gain.
The boy who used to be an escatsy has now emerged as lustful fantasy.
Taking care of mine, ensuring everytime I am fine. Running along silhouette, you transformed into my Amante.
From singing songs in farewell, your love bloomed on my gloomed gravel.
I know u don't love me and can't hope of enjambment of being we.
Dancing on the floor, I just enjoyed profound core.
Your hands on my waist made my bitter lips taste.
I won't forget you wishing the same Forbidding goodbye, please don't ask me why? Trust me u will sooner see me.

S. Vasha Varthini

S. Vasha Varthini is a Creative person with optimistic vibes. Working as assistant professor in Department of English. Love to new things always. Residing in coimbatore, Tamil Nadu. Explore the world through writings. Happy person with sheer enthusiasm.
Insta ID - dewdropzofmyheart

Crawl

Giggles sound sweeter
Step in foot on earth
Shaky dance moves on walk
Creepy sounds often
Repeat of same speech in startup talks
Faster moves here and there
Rolling of eyes to watch new things around
Mind speeds up with fraction of seconds
Words of them amuses sometimes
Gazing of them reduces stress lightens heart
With them home is fulfilled
Without them home is a house
Shouts to find it interesting
Silence show emptiness
Little things always find it happy
As little as children on earth

Pratima Yadav "Shaani"

Shaani... MBBS student and a part-time writer.
Quite passionate about reading novels and writing especially poetry and song lyrics.
Soon gonna be a published author.
Contact her at yadavpratimayaduvanshi@gmail.com
Instagram account @itsshaani

हवाओं की दास्तान बस हवाएं जानती हैं

ढलता सूरज है कि कल भी सुबह होगी का आगाम दे जाता है..ये
चांद है कि खामोंशियों में भी जाने कितने पैगाम दे जाता है...
कहने को तो ये किनारे भी बहुत कुछ कहते हैं
लहरों के होकर उन्हें रोक नहीं पाते हैं
कुदरत की कहानी कुछ को ही समझ आती है
कुछ बात है कि हवाओं की बस हवाएं जानती हैं
इक गुल भी जाने कितनी कहानियां कह जाता है
ये बारिश का पानी कितनों के आंसू छिपाता है
बहते पानी की खामोंशियां बहुत कुछ सिखाते हैं
झरनों के उफान दरिया में शान्त से बहते हैं
गमलों मे कैद पौधे की बेचैनी कुछ को ही समझ आती है.. कुछ बात
है कि हवाओं की बस हवाऐं ही जानती हैं
आंगन की तुलसी मुरझाने लगी है
इक नयी बयार जो आने लगी है
अब कंक्रीट के जंगलों का दौर है आया
यहां गंगा भी बोतलों मे बिकने लगी हैं
वो दीवार के दरार से निकलते पीपल की तड़प
"शानी" बस तुझे ही तो रुलाती है...
ये जो हवाओं की दास्तान है ...बस ये हवाएं ही जानती हैं....

Sanskriti Basu

Sanskriti is an introverted person, who takes pleasure in observing things very minutely. She tries to express her observations not through her speech, but through her writings. She tries to see the world through the colourful lens of imagination and aspires to show her perception to the world, as she perceives it.

I Travelled One Day

Just like Wordsworth,
I travelled one day;
Not to far-off lands though,
I just wanted to be gay.

I walked on a narrow path,
That took me to a stream.
The stream was bubbling and thriving,
And was making the fields green.

The greenery calmed my heart,
The stream washed my soul.
I felt inspired enough
To keep journeying through the dawn.

Beyond the fields
Was the rising Sun.
Looking sleepily from under the blanket of clouds,
He prepared to complete works undone.
He let out a big yawn
And the fields filled with light.
He greeted the birds,
And brought flowers to life.

Oh I travelled one day
And I had found heaven!
Birds were singing,
The flowers were blooming,
Leaves were rustling,
The breeze was whooshing,
And the stream was gurgling.

They created the perfect melody.

It was Nature's best therapy.
It sanctified my heart and soul.
I travelled one day,
And it made me whole.

Vishali. S

Vishali is a literature student. She wants to to use all opportunities to achieve her goals. She loves her mother very much. She is a spectacular girl. She wants to learn many things for her success. She wants to travel other countries.

Good Moments

Jack and rosy loved eachother to the core but their parents didn't accept their love.After a few months they admitted to their love and supported them.Jack decided to study and settled in his carrier before marriage afterthat they marry.Jack went to US for his higher studies after he daily make a call to her,after a few months rosy met with an accident.Then she recovered and returned to home but she lost her voice.Jack make a call to her but she didn't pickup the call because if he knows the incident he leave all his privilege and return to see her.so she think don't bother to him.After a few years passed rosy went to meet her colleague rini.she said to her that jack gave me an invitation card he decided to marry a girl.Rosy felt embrassed and saw the invitation there is rosy's name .Rosy got surprised and she glad to saw jack in that place.Jack cried and said to rosy that in these two years,I got petrified because I don't know about your situation at finally I finished my studies after that I got a job and my rosy too.If you are dump it doesn't matter.I will carry you in my life you are my soul . After that they got married and lead their life. With their parents support.

Moral: Waiting is a sign of true love. It doesn't lookout the outer appearance of the person.At the same time True to your parents don't cheat them.

Suma an Indian

A simple girl who has dreams, dreams about her country! Do something to make herself satisfied.

(1)

Sometimes problems also make us feel happy
They make us realise how strong we are ! How much confident we are !!

Difficulties are not more beautiful than our smile !
Problems are not stronger than our strength!

(2)

Those days were really awesome
Every day was adventurous
Everything was real
Everything was pure
my smile from heart
My happiness in my eyes
Wish to be child again
Live my childhood again

Giftson Jose

Giftson Jose is a passionate teacher works in cbse school, Maharastra. He is born and bought up in Kerala. Later he completed UG and PG and came to work as a professional teacher in Tamilnadu, Karnataka, AP and Maharastra. He is not only a teacher but also working as a Poet, Public Speaker, Motivator, Volunteer and Social Worker in many prestigious organizations. In 2019, MVLA Trust selected him as the best role model teacher of India. He has been a passionate supporter of initiatives that encourage students to seek the value of education.

My Memories

I'm in love with the sense of life,
Nor Joy with those sleepless nights
With all the skies were sunshine
And with the cooling splash of rain
Where the ripple dewdrops lies..

Behind every dark clouds of my Life,
Still rise up more dreams as looming
Those dreams always locked up tight for
The dreams once made scattered
With thought of own shattering cry..

Into the living sea of my life's esteems,
And even the winds of whispering smiles
I wish an ensure fun-fiilled days and nights
Melting in my warm days that I believe
My Memories, that none can take away..

The Full Moon

When I was sitting in the quietness
Some sound waves of vibrations came
Look up at the pretty shiny full moon
It's round as a silver selene sphere.

When I was looking in the night skies
It feels to notice that the glossy
Instead, I will concentrate that
Smile of your crystal ball shaped face.

When I was thinking in the darkness
It made me a little wonder sometimes
Even the darkest duskiness time also
Standing alone and shine it's hope of light.

When I was writing in the incessant thoughts
It tells the utter truth of our real life
Not everyone can't shine like a sun
Let's be a moon of our own dark times.

Durga Singh Thakur

He is in the process of making desire and determination meet to get the dream come true:)
Instagram: craving__love

(1)

I learnt to explain myself to anyone from my grandpa
He used to tell me
"The one who trust you don't except your explanation and the one who don't trust , won't believe your explanation ".

(2)

The letters were his asset
They said he was outdated
He smiled secretly
He knew those were written by her five decades ago .

Mansha Poddar

Mansha Poddar was born on 14th August 2003 in Sambalpur, Odisha. Since childhood her parents and teachers supported her in her writing skills. She is a sprouting bud of fantasy who loves to dress up her words. She aspires to become a well known writer as well as a Forest Officer. You can reach her for more of her scribbled writings on Instagram at @perpetual_covet

माँ

ममता और करूणा का सागर जो बरसाती है,
मेरे दुखी होने पर खुद रोने लग जाती है,

मेरे हर सुख दुख में जो मेरा साथ निभाती है,
अपने आंचल तले जो अपने बच्चों को सुलाती है,

अपनी छत्र छाया मैं जो अपने बच्चों को पालती है,
बड़ा करके एक अच्छा इंसान बनाती है,

उसकी हर मुश्किलों में उसकी ढा़ल बन खड़ी हो जाती है,
वो नारी ही जगत जननी हमारी मां कहलाती है!

लेखन मेरा जुनून है

लेखन मेरा जुनून है जो मेरा हौसला बढ़ाती है,
काग़ज़ और कलम के मिलते ही ख्यालों की बाढ़ ले आती है,

हर एक शब्द लिखते ही मेरे मन एक खुशी मिल जाती है,
मेरे मन में चल रहें विचारों को मेरी कलम कविता में बदल जाती है,

हर एक शब्द समाज को एक नयी राह दिखाती है,
लेखन खाली लिखना ही नहीं लेखन बदलाव को दर्शाती है,

लेखन एक कवि की जान और उसका सम्मान कहलाती है,
एक लेखन ही तो है जो मन के भावो को दर्शाती है,

लेखन कभी दीया रूपी बनकर किसी के जीवन को रोशन कर जाती है,
लेखन ही तो जो कागज़ और कलम का सही प्रयोग करना सिखाती है!

Deepti Bagde

Deepti Bagde is from Antagarh, dist-kanker (Chhattisgarh). She is a Co-author in 5 anthologies. she is an amazing writer. she wants to spread positivity in society through her pen.

मम्मी- पापा

जब भी मै हंसती हूं,आप मुस्कुराते हो।
ज़िन्दगी जीने का अंदाज़ मुझे सिखाते हो।
हार जाऊं गर खुद से भी, हौसला मुझे दिलाते हो।
भटक जाती राह तो, सही राह दिखाते हो।
देते मुझे ज़िन्दगी जीने की पूरी आजादी।
लगाते मुझपर कभी कोई रोक नहीं।
पूरे करते मेरी हर ख्वाहिश।
मानो आपके अपने कोई भी शौक नहीं।
इतना निः स्वार्थ प्रेम सिर्फ आप ही कर सकते हो।
पूरी दुनिया से मेरे लिए लड़ सकते हो।
मै मानती हूं खुद को खुशकिस्मत जो आपको मैने पाया है।
आपके रूप में ईश्वर मानो मेरे समक्ष प्रकट हो आया है।
आपके साथ मानो ज़िन्दगी मेरी,एक मधुर संगीत बन गई है।
मेरी दुनिया प्रेम , परवाह,अपनेपन के रंगों से रंग गई है।
संग आपके मेरा हर एक पल मानो त्यौहार है।
ग़म के लिए कोई जगह नहीं, खुशियां बेशुमार है।
कहने को है बहुत कुछ,पर आप जानते मेरे दिल कि हर एक बात हो।
मेरी ज़िन्दगी और खुशियों की वजह , मम्मी- पापा बस आप हो।

Vidhi Bhadreshbhai Desai

A teacher by profession and writer by passion Vidhi loves to pen down her feelings in simple words...

Childhood

How beautiful the Childhood was!
So many memories to recall.
That Morning walk and Evening play,
From Story books to Fiction plays.
I remember them each and everyday,
The days that I spent at my favorite place.
In my dreams they come now- a -days,
Tell me how beautiful were my childhood days.

मुझे फिरसे बच्चा होना हैं||

"बचपन मतलब मासुमियत जहा मेरी आँखों में थी,
बचपन मतलब जब सचाई मेरी बातो में थी!
बचपन मतलब वो छुट्टियों में ननिहाल की गलियों में खेल कर थक जाना,
नानी की गोद में सर रखकर सो जाना!
बचपन मतलब जहा हर ख़ुशी मुझे दोस्तों के साथ खेल कर मिलती थी,
और बचपन मतलब जब मेरी आँखे छोटी छोटी खुशियाँ ढूंढ़ती थी!
ना जाने कब उम्र बढ़ती गई,
वो ननिहाल की गलिया हमसे छूटती गई!
फस गए कहा इस जूठी दुनिया में,
सच हे जहा दूर कही एक छोटी सी पुड़िया में!
लोट के जाना है मुझे उस बचपन की दुनिया मे,
जहा सबकुछ है सच्चा जैसे जादू की दुनिया में!
छुप जाना है माँ के आँचल मे,
थाम कर पापा का हाथ साथ चलना है!
चुरानी है इमलियाँ दोपहर मे वो ननिहाल के पेडों से,
सुनाने है वो किस्से ,जिससे बच हम निकले!
आखिर में फिरसे भाई- बहेनो से गले लिपट कर रोना है,मुझे फिरसे बच्चा होना हैं!

Aarya Jha

A student, getting a step closer to " LIFE GOALS ". I was in the list of CBSE board exam toppers during my highschool days. A white Rose who never gets annoyed by cactus's opinion.

Summer Nights

Those late-night times
Spent with books gave me
some of the happiest moments.
Searching on Google,
spending hours on Assignments and projects.
Admiration and Appreciation bloomed.
Highest Marks brought
inner peace and bliss.
Those summer Nights and mini celebrations.
Cold coffee and starry night,
Taylor Swift and
Selena Gomez's songs on repeat.
Those summer Nights and
High school days.
That joy of becoming
House captain and class captain.
Dealing with haters and foes.
Conquering Obstacles and
Keeping my Crown safe.
Those summer Nights and
mini celebration.

Every page of the book of the fiction genre
is like a portal to a magical world.

Bloom like a bunch of pink bougainvilleas
Enchanting and captivating.

I am the kind of girl, who finds
the aroma of coffee more pleasing
than the sparkling diamonds.

Yashika Karamchandani

Yashika Karamchandani is a literature enthusiast who uses a pen as her way of expressing herself to the world. The young and ambitious seventeen-year-old has always chosen writing as her way to pour her heart out. The author of a recently published novel 'Dreams do come true', she'd taken her first step towards her dream. She is a dreamer and a strong believer in the fact 'Dreams do come true'.

Live What You Love

Life is all about just one moment, which demands to be lived to its fullest cause it lasts for just a moment.
Sometimes its okay to laugh on yourself when you fell down, sometimes learn to dance without any reason when you are happy, sometimes let yourself free to discover love and life in everything.
Find happiness in little things,
Spread happiness.
Smile and be the reason behind someone's smile each day,
Live what you love.

Live Laugh Love

Zindagi ko ek esi party ki tarah jeena chahiye ki jab maut aaye
to saath bethkar do drinks maarkar jaan lekar chali jaaye...
Life is all about experiences,
collect memories not things,
the world around us is waiting for us with its arms open,
all we need is to keep our hearts, minds and eyes always open
to welcome the unexpected.
Live life as if you were to die tomorrow,
enjoy every moment of life
cause life is all about just one moment, with infinite memories
which demands to be felt and enjoyed at that moment itself,
the world is full of love,
all we need to do is to embrace it,
world is full of beautiful people at every turn of life,
waiting to teach us a new lesson, a new meaning of life daily.
world is full of beautiful places,
waiting to be explored to give us memories which will remain
with us till our last breath.
So enjoy every moment of life,
laugh while you still have teeth,
be a reason behind others happiness
you have only one life
live what you love,
so on your last day you won't look back to your life with regret
smile at whatever life offers you,
and make all your dreams come true.

Ishwari Kishor Shirur

मी ईश्वरी किशोर शिरुर. अंबरनाथ येथे राहत असून परीघावरच्या कविता, अस्मिता आणि सुगंध सोबतीचा या काव्यसंग्रहात स्वलिखित कविता प्रकाशित झाल्या असून स्टोरी मिरर मध्ये माझ्या स्वलिखित कथेला Best Author Of The Week प्रमाणपत्र देऊन सन्मानित केले आहे. Ruiate आणि उत्तरायण मासिकांमध्ये लेख व कविता प्रकाशित झालेली आहे.

आकृती

कोऱ्या कागदावर माझ्या तु पेरला रंग आशेचा
तान्ह्या हातात माझ्या दिला ओंकार लेखणीचा

वात्सल्याचा प्रकाश तुझा दुरावल्या वासनेच्या वाटा
पुन्हा पुन्हा पदरात घेऊन कित्येक चुका तु माफ केल्या

तुला नसे आठ तासांची ड्युटी ना असे कधी सुट्टी
महिन्यातले ते चार दिवस तरी तु घेते का विश्रांती??

लोक सगळी म्हणतात आई होणं कठिण असतं
तुला पाहिल्यावर मात्र मला सगळंच सोप वाटतं

दुनियेत या देवाने घडवली एक गजब आकृती
दैव माझे मला तु आई म्हणून याजन्मी लाभली

माऊली तू जगताची विणते गुंतलेले धागे सारे
कुशीत घेते पिलांना जशी सारी तुझीच लेकरे

Kanupriya Rastogi

She is Kanupriya Rastogi. From Bareilly UP. Writing is her hobby and when the hobby turns into passion, it will rock. She thinks writting is the best way to release emotions............

क्या तुम्हे याद है??????

क्या तुम्हे याद है कि जब घंटों तक वो तुम्हारी बेफिजूल की बाते तुम जबरदस्ती मुझे सुनाया करते थे............
क्या तुम्हे याद है वो मेरे एक फोन कॉल पर तुम भले है कितना भी थके हुए या रात भर के जगह होने के बाद भी कैसे कॉलेज आ जाया करते थे,,
क्या तुम्हे याद है वो मुझे दिया हुए तुम्हारा पहला तोहफा?
वो एक गुलाब तुम सुभा सुभा ना जाने कहां से के आए थे,
वो उसे देखकर मेरा चेहरा भी कैसे खिल गया था ना?
आज भी वो गुलाब मेरी किताबों में महफूज रखा है
अक्सर मै उसे देखती हूं जब जब भी तेरी याद आती है.......
और उस सूखे गुलाब से आज भी जाना तेरी उंगलियों की खुशबू आती है.........
बताओ ना या क्या तुम्हे याद है अब भी वो जब तुम तंग आकर मुहब्बत से अपनी, अक्सर मेरे पास आकर हमारी यारी में वो सुकून दा पाया करते थे.......
एक शब्द भी कोई के से अगर मेरे बारे में तुम जबरदस्ती उससे मेरे लिए लड़ जाया करते थे........
क्या तुम्हे याद है वो देखकर उदास मुझे तुम अपने सारे गम भुलाकर सिर्फ मुझे हंसाया करते थे,
हां मुझे आज भी ये सारी बाते बहुत अच्छे से याद हैं यार
अक्सर सोचकर इन्हे मेरा दिल भी बड़ा सुकून सा पाता है,
मगर सच कहूं अगर तो ए यार सचमुच हार बस मेरी जान ले जाता है सवाल कि,
जिसे हर लम्हा मै सोचती रहती हूं, फकत मै ही मुन्तजिर हूं अपने यार की प्रिया! या कभी कभी तन्हाई में गलती से उसको भी मेरा खयाल आता है...............

Aishwarya Garg

Aishwarya is a dental student by profession and a writer by passion. She has co-authored a few anthologies. She loves expressing her feelings in words and wants to become an influencer in the future.

बीती यादें

कुछ यादें पुरानी आती है
फिर ताज़गी भर जाती है
कुछ खुशी उन लम्हों की
हल्की सी मुस्कान दे जाती है।

वो बारिश की बूंदे
वो पंछी की गूंजे
वो बिगड़े सुरो का तराना
अपनो से मिलने पर ना रहता खुशी का ठिकाना।

मां का गले लगाना पापा से मजाक में लड़ जाना।
कुछ बेजुबानों को अपना यार बनाना
और बगीचे के फूल खिलाना।
अकेले में मेरा खुद से ही मिल जाना
रंगो से सजी एक दुनिया बनाना।
एक महफ़िल की शान अकेले ही बड़ाना
अच्छा लगता है यह किस्सा पुराना।

घूमना नई जगह पहाड़ों का सुकून पाना।
चुपके से मेरा कुछ कर जाना
हस्ते हस्ते यूहीं गिर जाना
गम में भी खुशी का बहाना बनाना
अब याद आता है मुझे वो गुजरा जमाना।

अतरंगी सा है मेरा खज़ाना
कदमों की अपने छाप बनाना
फिर उन्ही जज्बातों से चित्र सजाना
यादों को बस सहेजते जाना

नए नए कुछ खेल बनाना
ऐसा था मेरा बचपन सुहाना।

शामे कुछ गर्मियों की खास है
कुछ लोगों के बिना मेरा जीवन आजाद है।
अच्छे कुछ लम्हे यह याद है
इन यादों से दुनिया आबाद है।

Priya Jha

Priya Jha hails from Madhubani (Mithilanchal) Bihar. She is pursuing her masters from accountancy honours. Apart from this, she is well known for her teaching, painting, and poetry skills.
Currently, she is one of the core members of Speakup Mithila, a literature community-based in Bihar.

तुम्हारा आना

तुम मेरी जिंदगी में ठीक उस तरह से आये जैसे कि ग्रीष्म ऋतु के बाद वर्षा ऋतु आती है,
कैसे गर्मी से बेहाल , धूप से परेशान , तपती दोपहरी में जलने के उपरांत लोगों में खुशी की लहर दौड़ जाती है बारिश की बूंद परते ही,
कैसे दिन रात एक किसान दुआ मांगता है गर्मी के बाद बारिश के आने की, और कैसे उसके चेहरे पे खुशी की लहर दौड़ जाती है, बारिश की पहली बून्द परते ही,
ठीक वैसी ही खुशी, वैसा ही सुकून मुझे तुम्हारे आने से मिली थी,
कैसे छोटे बच्चों में कौतूहलता होती है गर्मी की छुट्टीयों में कही दूर घूमने जाने की,
ठीक वैसी ही कौतूहलता थी मुझे जिंदगी के हर सुख दुख में तुम्हे मेरा सहभागी बनाने की,
हाँ, मैं मानती हूँ कि तुम अपने मर्जी से आये थे, और गए भी अपनी मर्जी से,
लेकिन क्या एक आखिरी अलविदा तक तुम्हे मुझसे कहते नही बना,
न खबर, न पता, कुछ भी तो नही पता है मुझे तुम्हारा,
आज भी चांद से हजारों बातें करती हूँ तुम्हारी,
एकांत मन से कमरे की दिवाली पे लगी खूंटी और उसमें टंगी हमारी एकलौती साथ वाली तश्वीर को घंटों तक निहारती हूँ,
पुकारती हूँ तुम्हे मैं हर उस दरमियाँ जब मुझसे आशुओं के भार सहे नही जाते,
देखो न, पिछली बरसात में हम साथ ही तो थे,
एक ही छतरी में पूरा शहर माप लिया करते थे,
गर्मी की तपती दोपहरी में भी हाथों में हाथ डाल मिलों तय कर लिया करते थे,
अब बस ये ग्रीष्म ऋतु बीतने ही वाली है,
मुझे इंतजार है अब भी तुम्हारा,
हो सके तो अबके बरसात में लौट आना।

Lakshmi Soni

She belongs to The city of oranges, Nagpur, Maharashtra. Instagram - @dil_ki_kalm__

वो नदिकिनारे शाम ....
ठंडी पवन... निला आसमां....
पीले से छोटे- छोटे फूल.....
हरितीमा की चादर.... फैली चारों ओर....
खूबसूरती का ना कोई ओर ना कोइ छोर....
पत्तों की सरसराहट... पानी की खलखालहट....
दूध सा बहता झरना....
कांच सा कंचन पानी....
उसमें अठखेलियां करती मछलियों की रानी..
मखमली घास... संग ओस की बूंदों का साथ
गीतों की बारात.....पंछियों की चेहचाहट.....
पाषाण से टकराता.....
मिट्टी की बाहों में समाता....
दुनियां भुला बहता चला आता....
घाट- घाट की ठोकरें खाता.....
फ़िर भी मिलने दौड़ा चला आता......
सौगात में सबकी प्यास बुझाता......
ये किमती पल..... तुम्हारा मेरा साथ....
काश!! यही थम जाता.....
पर याद जब भी आता ......
लबों पर मुस्कुराहट बिखेर जाता.....
यादों का कारवां और ये सिलसिला यूं ही चलते जाता.....
मन को यादों से भर,, उन पलों को जगा जाता..
'दास्तां - ए - शाम' सुना जाता है।।।

Wo pyaari si yaadein.....
Teri - meri haseen mulakatein.....
Wo Barrish ki cham-cham ......
aur nadaan si batein....
Wo Nasamjh se wadein......
Wo ulfat ki shararatein......
Tiffin tera khane ka khajana....
Basta tera sare school ka tehkhana.....
Baton ki budiyaan.....
Style ki gudiyaan ...
Sabki nani,,, sabse sayani .....
Dikhne me Masum .....
Shararto me ustaad.....
Balo ka shaokeen ....doston ki jaan....
Har kaand ka neta....
Tarkeeb ki dukaan.....
Wo killing muskurahat...
Tere aane ki sarsarahat.....
Na aaj ki chinta..... Na kal ki fikr....
Dil ka garden,, aur sapno ka jahan....
Smile bekher deta hain....
Aaj bhi teri yaadon ka silsila .....
Mere dil ke tehkhane me .....
Yaadon ke saayein me ....
humesha mere pass hain tu...
Humesha mere saath hain tu .....
Meri pyari si muskurahat me

R. Susanna Celsia

Passionate writer, blogger, and poet who has published her solo book "oasis of poetry", who not only writes fictions with allegories and metaphors but blends them with reality

Summer has always been the favorite time of the year, as a child, the happiest part was staying home for summer vacations and doing all like, having no one to tell me what to do, no early mornings no school, no homework no stress, I loved watching "popeye the sailor man" as I ate my favorite breakfast pesarattu and red chutney and afternoons will watch Asterix and Obelix and evening was my favorite time to head to the park, watch the fountain, play in the swing and play endlessly in the mud as my mother would work out. As I grew older summer vacations was my most favorite part like always I loved going to my grandmother's house fighting with my cousins and trying new stuff, like mixing up fevicol and paper and trying to make dough out of it, starting a beauty salon with my dolls, puzzle books, coloring books, and tv.

I loved going to the beach and chilling and loved eating ice cream, sometimes it was reading a novel and listening to music as an adult I loved having moonlight dinner with cousins with mangos season with spices and mango sambar and endless icecream and juice and long rides in the highways, even though we don't have summer vacations now I always love summer.

Kalamkaar

This is Kalamkaar. He is from Uttrakhand bought up in Meerut(Up). His hobbies are reading and writing. His interest is in writing. He loves writing. He is part of 295 +Anthologies as Co-Author. He won 290 + Certificate in Writing, He Starts writing on 29 February 2020. He is part of 2 anthologies as Co-Author going for the record and He is omg record holder as Co-Author of the Book Called Laposia. He is part of 4 international Anthologies as Co-Author. He is a simple and people observer. His insta handle is kalamkaar51 and his email is kalamkaar51@gmail.com. He believes in Karma.

गर्मियों की छुट्टियां

गर्मीया में कालिया सारी खिल जाती हैं!
आइसक्रीम और बर्फ का गोला साथ अपने लाती हैं!
खुश होते हैं बच्चे छुट्टियां उनकी पड़ जाती हैं
नानी के घर में बच्चे जाते हैं, गाँव के खाने का ज़ायका में लेते हैं!
लस्सी पी कर मुँछ अपनी बनाते हैं नानी को दिखाते हैं!
पेड़ में लगे झूले खेलने जाते है, तेराकी करने नदियों में जाते हैं!
खेलते हैं दिन भर और हल्ला पुरे घर में मानते हैं!
बच्चे सारे मिलकर गुल्फी खाके आते हैं!
अगले दिन सुबह उठकर आँगन में लगे झूला खेलने चले जाते हैं!
खाते में जाकर आम तोड़कर लाते हैं!
सारे दिन पेड़ो में चढ़कर अमरुद, आम आदि सब खाते हैं!
खेलते हैं सारे भाई बहन घर नहीं वो कई बार बुलाने पे नहीं आते हैं!
हो जाती हैं छुट्टियां खतम कुछ दिनों बाद यादे लेके वहाँ से जाते हैं!
प्रेम और आशीर्वाद की सोगद नानी के वहाँ से लेके जाते हैं!
बिछड़ते हैं भाई बहन नयन में अश्रु भर के विदा करते जाते हैं!
और दोबारा छुट्टियों में वापस आने का वादा देके जाते हैं!

Sarvesh Bagde

This is Sarvesh Bagde, Hailing from "The City of Oranges" Nagpur, Maharashtra. He is a student of life sciences presently pursuing B.Sc Biotechnology from Shri Shivaji Science College, Nagpur. Writing is his passion and he is penning for the last 5 years. He loves writing Quotes, articles, some short stories, etc.

That's not giving you a lot of detail, is it?

Follow him at

Blogs-https://sarveshbagde.blogspot.com/?m=1

YourQuote-https://www.yourquote.in/sarveshbagde

खुशी का एहसास !

"ये तेरा घर ये मेरा घर
किसी को देखना हो गर
तो पहले आ के माँग ले,
मेरी नज़र तेरी नज़र
ये तेरा घर ये मेरा घर
ये घर बहुत हसीन है ......"

पुराने ज़माने के गाने हमेशा मन में एक नई उमंग और हौसला भर देते है !
जावेद अख़्तरजी द्वारा लिखित यह गीत इसी बात का एक जीता जागता स्वरूप है ।

प्रस्तुत गीत में जावेदजी ने यह बड़ी सफाई से दर्शाया है कि नज़र से ज़्यादा किसी व्यक्ति का नज़रिया बेहतर हो तो वह कुछ भी हासिल कर सकता है ।

सब कुछ पाया है मैंने, हासिल कुछ भी नहीं ख्वाहिशें है मुकम्मल, कामिल कुछ भी नहीं।

अगर आपके जीवन में संतोष ना हो तो सब कुछ होने के बाद भी पर्याप्त कुछ नहीं होगा !
जीवन की छोटी छोटी चीजों में ही खुशी ढूंढ़ना असली जीवन की परिभाषा है।

अब भाई हमने तो अपनी खुशी एक छोटी गरम चाय की प्याली में सजा रखी है । उसे ही पिते पिते इस गाने को सुनकर स्वर्गीय अनुभूति का हम भोग ले रहे है।
आप भी आगे सुनिए !

"जो चाँदनी नहीं तो क्या, ये रोशनी है प्यार की
दिलों के फूल खिल गये, तो फ़िक्र क्या बहार की
हमारे घर न आयेगी, कभी खुशी उधार की
हमारी राहतों का घर, हमारी चाहतों का घर
ये तेरा घर ये मेरा घर ये घर बोहोत हसीन है ...."

Rashmi Baweja

रश्मी इस कहानी की लेखिका बिल्कुल अपने नाम के अनुरूप ही सबके जीवन को प्रकाशित करती है। रश्मी हरियाणा के सोनीपत जिले की निवासी है। उन्होंने MCA किया है। उन्होंने अपना लेखन कार्य 2016 में प्रारंभ किया। वे बहुत ही स्पष्ट वादी है।वे फेसबुक पर HEART TOUCHING पेज पर भी लिखती हैं।https://www.facebook.com/rashmibaweja1993/अलग अलग विषयों पर वे बहुत अच्छा लिखती हैं। उनकी रचनाएँ पढ़कर दिल को सुकून मिलता है।

बचपन के दिन

बचपन के वो दिन आज भी याद आते है।
वो प्यारे प्यारे पल आज भी मुझे सताते है।

माँ बाप से अपनी हर फरमहिशे पूरी करवाते थे।
छोटी छोटी बात पर रूस कर खूब नखरे उठवाते थे।

अपने मन की हर बात अपनो को बताते थे।
चेहरे पर झूठी हँसी रखकर नही मुस्कुराते थे।

दुनियाँ के बीच शहजादे बनकर सब पर हुकुम चलाते थे।
उन गुड्डे गुड़ियों के बीच अपना बचपन बिताते थे।

कहानियां सुनने के लिए दादी नानी को जगाते थे।
जब सो जाएं वो तो उन्हें नींद से उठाते थे।

बारिश की बूंदों पर छप छप कर नाचते थे।
पानी मे कागज़ की कश्तियां बनाकर तैराते थे।

मस्ती में खेल खेल कर सपको खूब सताते थे।
सबके लाडले सबके प्यारे बनकर अपनी हर जिद पूरी करवाते थे।

सुनहरे पल

तुम्हारे साथ बिताए हर पल सुनहरे थे।
ज़िन्दगी के हर पल में तुम साथ रहते थे।

हर वक़्त तुम मेरा हाथ थामे रहते थे।
दुनिया की हर चीज़ से तुम मुझे बचाते थे।

मेरे जिक्र में तुम हर वक़्त मौजूद रहते थे।
मेरी एक आवाज़ से तुम दौड़े चले आते थे।

हर वक़्त हम दूर होकर भी एक दुजे के पास रहते थे।
किसी एक भी तकलीफ हो तो बिना कहे समझ जाया करते थे।

दुनिया की भीड़ में बिना देखकर पहचान लिया करते थे।
आँखों से नही दिल की धड़कन से देख लिया करते थे।

तेरे साथ रहकर तकलीफ में भी खुश रहते थे।
दुख में तुम हाथ जो थाम लिया करते थे।

मेरे दर्द को तुम अपना दर्द समझते थे।
उस वक़्त में तुम मुझे अपने प्यार से हँसाया करते थे।

मालूम नही था ये वक़्त इतनी जल्दी बदल जायेगा।
जिसमे तुम कभी छोड़ के ना जाने के वादे करते थे।

Arkapriya Ghosh

Arkapriya Ghosh is about to graduate from high school..she's a writer of myth and fantasy..she's a good artist and a singer too...

Salen lee-The everlasting summer

I was surprised on waking up to see that Isha, my college friend was not there in the
room. Because of the lockdown, Isha could not return back to Chennai where she lives. So I
had invited Isha to stay with me until flight service was restored back. I have lived in Shimla
all through my life. So I was worried how Isha would find her way back. While I was busy
worrying, I heard the screech of my garden gate and Isha walked in. I was shocked to see
leaves tangled in her hair. I asked her where she had been, to which she replied that she had
come across a wonderful house and was there only. Just then a man passing by on hearing her retort stopped by introducing himself as Mr.Lucas.I felt that I had seen him somewhere but couldn't remember.
Lucas uncle said that the house which Isha had visited was a most amazing
scientific place.He said that the place was actually the home of famous Astronomer Salen
Lee but he was killed by some Indian soldiers on a warm summer day as he tried to teach the children of India for
free and make the children's life bright like the sun.Salen Lee had designed his house to teach poor children and had equipped his house
in such a way too.Just them Isha showed us a diary and to which Lucas uncle asked us to
read it and to try to educate children as much as we can.I asked him, "How can we educate
them? where will we get books?".He said that help was given by Salen Lee who tried to fulfill
his wishes.He advised us to visit the house of Salen Lee. With these words, he walked off.

After breakfast, we both decided to go to the house of Salen Lee.The house was completely covered with wild grass and the gate was rusty."It looks like a ghastly house, which was very beautiful once."I said.As soon as I entered the house I was captivated by its inner beauty. It was filled with books and toys. I understood that we can easily educate children here.I asked Isha to take out the diary.The last page was a picture titled Salen Lee with a picture. Horror registered on my face as I looked towards Isha and she said, "Lucas uncle??Who did we meet then." Lucas uncle's words rang out in our minds".Help will be given by Salen Lee to those……..

IT WAS A SUMMER DAY!!

Moumita Bagchi

लेखिका मौमिता बागची, कलकत्ता के प्रेसीडेन्सी कालेज से हिन्दी साहित्य में एम° ए° हैं। उन्होंने 2019 में बी° एड° की डिग्री हासिल की। साथ ही वे एक प्रशिक्षित हिन्दी अनुवादक और कान्टेन्ट राइटर भी हैं।

भारत सरकार के दो उपक्रमों के राजभाषा विभाग में कुछ वर्षों तक कार्य करने का इनका अनुभव है।

इनकी दो प्रकाशित पुस्तकें:- 1) कुछ अनकहे अल्फ़ाज़ कुछ अधूरे ख्वाब (,2019), 2) माँ की डायरी (2020)

मैं प्यासी, तुम सागर

आज सुबह से ही शिल्पी का मन बहुत दुःखी था। नहीं, कोई नई बात नहीं थी। शादी के ठीक एक हफ्ते के अंदर ही एक अक्सीडेन्ट के कारण उसकी एक टांग को काटना पड़ गया था। और इसके साथ ही सात साल का लंबा उसका पत्रकारिता का कैरियर भी अंत हो गया था। इतने वर्षों के बाद भी रह- रहकर यही बात उसे उदास कर देता था!

और जब भी वह उदास होती तो अपनी डायरी निकालकर बैठती थी। अपने भावों को लिपिबद्ध करके ही उसके मन को शांति मिलता था। उसका पति रौनक यद्यपि उसका बहुत ख्याल रखता था।उसका दुःख बाँटने का भी काम किया करता था और साथ ही भाँति- भाँति के साँत्वना से शिल्पी का मन बहलाने की कोशिश करता था।

रौनक जानता था कि शिल्पी को जो बिमारी है वह शारीरिक कम और मानसिक ज्यादा है। क्योंकि अपनी शारीरिक विकलांगता को तो शिल्पी ने मन से मान लिया था, परंतु उसका जो मन था वह हमेशा बड़ा विचलित रहा करता था---!

शादी के दस साल बाद भी वे दोनों माता- पिता न बन पाए थे। इसमें शिल्पी का अनाग्रह ही अधिक था। वह बहुत डरती थी माँ बनने से। इसलिए भी उनके जीवन में अपार खालीपन व्याप्त था।

शिल्पी अपने कार्यालय के संपादक विभाग में काम करती थी। मतलब कि उसे आउटडोर काम नहीं करने होते थे। उसे और भी कई सारे ऑफर आए थे काम के, परंतु एक दो इंटरव्यू के बाद वह घर से बाहर जाने को राज़ी न हुई।

आजकल वह दिनभर डायरी में न जाने क्या लिखा करती थी। किसी से ज्यादा बोलती चालती भी नहीं।

पिछले मार्च में ला◌ॅकडाउन के समय रौनक ने उसके लिए एक लैपटा◌ॅप खरीदकर दिया और स्टडी रूम के एक कोने को सजाकर शिल्पी के लिए उसका अपना राइटिंग कार्नर बना दिया।

आजकल शिल्पी ज्यादातर समय यहीं बिताया करती थी!

आठ महीने बाद।

शिल्पी का आज जन्मदिन था। इस दिन का कोई विशेष महत्व न था उसके लिए।अक्सीडेन्ट के बाद से उसने सारे सेलिब्रेशन्स से अपने आपको अलग कर लिया था।
दोपहर से ही सरदी भी बहुत बढ़ गई थी। रोज़ की तरह वह चुपचाप आकर राइटिंग डेस्क पर जा बैठी थी। कई रोज़ से उसकी प्यारी डायरी उसे नहीं मिल रही थी। उसी को ढूँढने में वह व्यस्त थी कि तभी डोरबेल की आवाज़ उसके कानों पर पड़ी।
शिल्पी के नाम से कोई पार्सल आया था। उसे कौन पार्सल भेजेगा यह सोचते हुए उसके हाथ तेजी से पार्सल खोलने में लग गए थे।
रौनक आज घर पर ही था। उसने आकर टीवी चला दिया।
विज्ञापन में अपना नाम सुनकर शिल्पी चौंकी। उसके द्वारा लिखित किताब का एक विज्ञापन टीवी पर आ रहा था। पर उसने तो कोई पुस्तक प्रकाशित ही नहीं करवाई थी?! फिर???
उसने आश्चर्य से रौनक की ओर देखा। रौनक ने उसके हाथ में पड़े पार्सल की ओर इशारा किया।

Krishna Motwani

Krishna Motwani is a Student currently. She uses it to pen down her feelings. She is a moody girl.
She started writing in the month of June 2020.
She writes in her free time. She writes some motivational quotes or poetry too and practices artworks also. She lives her life like a bird
As the bird flies freely and enjoys life like that she also lives her life freely and enjoys fullest.
For motivating and inspiring poems and quotes, you can check her on instagram: @ unique__blog_

Vibes!

I always use to talk with the moon at night to get some peace, I share every moment of the day with moon and you know whenever I talk to moon, I usually see that hidden smile of the moon which teaches me to keep smiling always and fight with your problems with hope and smile!

It was 5 pm, I was walking on the street. I was bit sad that day, so I decided to spend some time with nature. Suddenly fast breeze came, leaves started falling from trees, all the birds were chirping. It was merry and cold weather, all of the people went home and I was alone on the street, was feeling the fragnant of the air. It was like, nature too don't me to be sad. It just given me peace and changed my mood, removed all of my stress. It was the nature's beauty, I felt that day. It was the best day of my life. I was too sad from morning but these 1 - 2 hours made my day!

It were the best vibes ever! I can't forget that day till my last breath!

Hema Kirthiga J

She is Hema Kirthiga J, and her pen name is sparkle. She is professionally a psychologist and passionately a writer. She heals others but writing heals her. She is a writer, reader, orator, and believer. She is from Chennai. She lives by the principle of inspiring and be inspired. You can reach her at
Instagram- @the_pen_queen
Email- inker.sparkle@gmail.com
Your quote – JKM

The Best Moments Of My Life!

You,
Its all you,
Who created my beat moments,
Who brought sunshine into my life,
Who loved me unconditional,
Who sat with me through endless nights,
Who was never impatient,
Those days of ours,
Is all that I have,
With you by my side,
Having endless chatters,
Looking into each other's eyes,
And understanding what one feels,
Passing the days with love,
Struggling along with each other,
Those days spent in the canteen,
With good food and good life,
With a little more essence if love,
Helping each other,
Through thick and thin,
Those memories,
Still remains fresh in my heart.

Diksha Motwani

Diksha is a passionate girl from Mumbai, Maharashtra. She loves to pen her feelings. She is an introvert but her pen makes her extrovert. She is a writer, singer, artist, and poet!

Still am waiting!

You promised that you will be back very soon,
But you didn't,
I attempted to forget you as you were maybe a boon,
But I didn't!

Yes, you are still my morning's first thought,
Yes, I still adore you,
Yes, I still love you.
But may be now, I will not have you.

You were my blooming moon,
You were my shine of darkest days,
unfortunately, you are not mine now,
Yet I still wait for you every single day!

Gautam Balasaheb Kardile

This is Gautam, Born on 27 November 2002. And 18 years old. From childhood, he is an all-rounder in every field. He is a free-verse poet, Coauthor of many anthologies, Dancer, Author, Elocutionist, Writer, and an academic topper now studying at Fergusson College, Pune. He dreams to be an all-rounder as he is preparing for MBBS and side by side working in short films and plays.

प्रेम पाहावं करून..

कधीतरी मलाही वाटतं
माझंही कोणीतरी असावं,
जिची आठवण आली तर
मन हू खुदकन हसावं।।१।।

कधीतरी मलाही वाटतं
माझ्याही मिठीत कोणीतरी निजावं,
तिने प्रेम नाही केलं तरी चालेल
पण एखादं निखळ हास्य नियमित दिसावं।।२।।

कधीतरी मलाही वाटतं
माझ्यावरही कोणीतरी हलकसं रुसावं,
तिला मनवता नाही आलं तरी चालेल
किमान मी तरी मलाच फसवावं।।३।।

कधीतरी मलाही वाटतं
मलाही कोणीतरी प्रेमाने जवळ घ्यावं,
ती दररोज भेटली नाही तरी चालेल
पण तिच्या आठवणींमध्ये तिचं प्रेम नक्की भासावं।।४।।

मी ही

अवघड चंचल वळणावरती
फसव्या सहानुभूतींचे फटकारे पडतील,
मी ही बिंधास्त अंगावर घेईन
आमुच्या यशाचे नवखे वारे सुटतील।।१।।

कवडीमोल भावना आमुच्या
डोळ्यांवाटे बरसू पाहतील,
मी ही आनंदाने नाहून घेऊन
नकळत आमुच्या अस्तित्वाचे निखारे फुलतील।।२।।

कधी अस्तित्वाला अग्नी देऊन
ते दशक्रियेच्या पंगतीला बसतील,
मी ही पोटभर जेवून घेईन
आता मात्र कर्तृत्वाचे अगणित तुषार उडतील
अगणित तुषार उडतील।।३।।

Varsha Fatakale Warade

मी ठाणे येथे राहते. मी व्यवसायाने परिचारिका आहे. मला गायन, वाचन आणि लिखाणाची खूप आवड आहे. कवितेच्या सर्व प्रकारात मी लिहीत असते. (हायकू, द्रोण काव्य, अष्टाक्षरी, दशाक्षरी गझल, चारोळी आणि इतरही सर्व प्रकार) माझे सर्वात आवडते काव्यप्रकार गजल आणि शायरी हे आहेत.कथा, ललित लेख, अलक कथा देखील लिहिल्या आहेत.खूप कविता वर्तमान पेपर, ई-बुक, आणि दिवाळी अंक यामध्ये छापून आल्या आहेत. साहित्यक्षेत्रात मला शंभरहून अधिक प्रमाणपत्र देखील मिळाली आहेत.

धागे संवेदनांचे

धागे संवेदनांचे उलगडून जात आहे
आर्तता मनाची मजला ज्ञात आहे
जखमा या जरी दिसल्या नाही तुला
हसूनी सगळे तिजला गोंजारून जात आहे

चांदण्यांची नक्षी अंबरात ही सजत आहे
लक्ष ताऱ्यात एक तारा तुटून जात आहे
नसे भान कोणास जरी ते तुटणे
इच्छा पुर्ततेची त्यात वेगळी बात आहे

जगणे झाले कठीण म्हणूनी मना ह्या खंत आहे
मैफिली सुखाच्या सजल्या जरी वेड्या मना एकांत आहे
गायले मीच गीत एकटीने तु बदलला प्रांत आहे
मिटतील जीवनाचे फास म्हणूनी हा आक्रांत आहे

दुःख असता डोंगराएवढे तरीही हसून जात आहे
निराशेच्या खोल गर्तेतून मी तारून जात आहे
जाऊन प्रश्नाच्या मुळाशी उत्तरे शोधत आहे
येतील जरी वादळे कितीही तरीही मी शांत आहे

पहिलं प्रेम विसरता येत का?

ठोकर मारली जरी तू पण
तुला विसरणं कठीण जातं
तू रंगविली स नाटक
पण मी प्रेम केलं होतं

कितीही यत्न केले तरी
पहिले प्रेम विसरता येते का?
तोडूनी मनाचे भावबंध असे
उगीच खोटे जगता येते का?

जोडीले सूर श्वासांचे
क्षणभंगुर का असेना
सजली मैफिल प्रेमाची
हृदय दूर का असेना

तव प्रीतीत मी चिंब भिजले
स्वप्न अबोली नयनी गुंफले
भावनाची ना कदर तुजला
हा डाव मी अर्ध्यावरी हरले

हारलेली बाजी जीवनाची
पुन्हा नव्याने जिंकता येते का?
असंख्य झाले वार हृदयावर
पुन्हा कधी ते सांधता येते का?

Shivani Bhardwaj

Student.

Feel Good Moments

My mood become good
When I remember you;
My eyes desire to see
Your portrait it keeps near my bed.
I feel good moments every morning
I know we are different,
But you're the my life
Whenever I was feel lonely
Just scooted on tiptoe and
Keep my forehead in your lap.
I feel like ' heaven'.
I feel good moments with you ' maa'.
You scold me on my mistake.
You proud me on my achievements.
But it's possible b'coz of you "maa".
And I feel good with you.
When I remember spend humorist time with you,
Can't be control my nonchalantly laughing.
Sometime we argue on silly topics,
Sometime we laugh on silly topics.
I feel good.
If the society against me,
I know you will with me and protect.
I feel good .
In the world everyone need special
Person to judge them and for caring.
But in my life you are,
You are always care me.
Sometime you become my motivator.
Spend time with you maa
Like being on vacation.
I feel refreshing, recharging,
And come stamina to face this crazy world.

I'll be live anywhere,
Your nonstoping conversation and advise always influential in my mind it follow by heart.
I feel good to think that;
You always with me.
You are just made for me.
Love you maa.

Amir Javed

Basically an introvert who is just fond of to reach the next heights of success...

The Story Of A Broken Heart

The story of a broken heart
Today I am writing because we are apart
Because expressing the thoughts can't repair but can heal the broken heart
I remembwr the day when you went away
Because after that I didn't find a way
We can't change what destiny has done
Everyone is enjoying our breakup as a means of fun
I am happy to see you with another one away
As it is your life you can live it on your own way
I am happy you jave moved on in your life
But there's a pain in heart which struck me with knife
I am trying to move on, but it is possible never
I love you and will keep lo ving till my whole life forever......

Priyanka Ramakant Kadam

She writes from heart what you relate and her heart says.
She feels every moment of life that she pen down through her writing which she felt with the heart.
Professionally she wants to be a developer but her dreams are so big and one of her dream is to explore as a writer as it inspires her alot towards the journey of her better life.
She loves to explore more and more...That's what her life is….

शहर की रात
वो दिन वो शाम ,
वह जीवन वो दुनिया ,
यह बहुत खूबसूरत है ....,
बस खुदसे प्यार करो
और खुलके मुसकुराते जियो...
उस शहर के रात इंतजार में ,
चांदनी आसमान में,
चमकते चांद में ,
जीवन के हर अच्छे पलों को महसूस करो
क्योंकि जीवन के हर
चीजों को देखा नहीं जा सकता
इसे आपको महसूस करना होगा ,
उस हर एक पलों में जीना होगा...
बस जीवन से प्यार करो
भुला के गम सारे दिल से जियो
हर बात में खुश रहो
उन हर एक पलों में खुलके जिओ...
और ढेर सारे बहुत यादें बनाओ..
तभी आप जीवन में कुछ नया पाओगे..

Jayashree Sahoo

Jayashree Sahoo is a habitant of Odisha.

Her writings started on yourquote, notojo, and mirakee like writing platforms. You can search her on yourquote by name of Jaya Jayashree. Nowadays She is member of many writing communities and earned a lots of certificates through her writings.

She is the Co.author of 160+ anthologies. Also She is Compiler of many anthologies in Hindi, English, and Odia languages. Currently, She is working as a project head and board member of a reputed publication.

Moments Are Memories

.

All moments are memories in our mind,
Maybe there bad or good,
But moments are always special,
When you spend your time with nature with your favourite person,
You feel so awesome,
You feel that moments musings
You want to remind these moments forever,
And you also doing this,
For memorising and mesmerizing everyday,
So moments not limited in just time limit,
Moments are always memories in our mind ...
Which unend ,
Uncountable ..

Archana Paryani

Archana Paryani - She is fervent fan of honor loyalty and chivalry. She brings life in the world where men and women stand shoulder to shoulder, steady in the desire to make the world a better place for all.
She is small town girl with bring big dreams. She is the perfect mixture of sweetheart and warrior.
She is a finance professional with a passion for writing.

Instagram handle : little_love_left

Yaad Hai Mujko

Yaad hai mujko
Vo kaise aa kar bass gale lag jati thi
Aur mere badan ki saari aag buuj jaati thi..

Yaad hai mujko
Jab jab mera haath tha sabne choda
Tab bass uss hi ne mera saath na choda..

Yaad hai mujko
Vo kis tarah dunia bhula kar mere paas aati thi
Aur aa kar meri puri dunia bann jati thi..

Yaad hai mujko
Vo kaise meri saari galtiyo parr parda daal kar
Meri harr haar ko jeet mein badal daalti thi..

Yaad hai mujko
Uska vo pagalpan wala pyaara sa junoon
De jata tha humesha mere dil ko sukoon..

Yaad hai mujko, Lekin...
Lekin.... yaad bhi hai na tujko?

Deepjyoti Chowdhury

Deepjyoti Chowdhury embraces reading and writing as her escape from the real world as well as a window to it. She is a strong believer of Christ and Karma. Currently pursuing Master's in English literature, she has written in 100+ anthologies, she is the author of "Heartfelt musings" and "The staircase to freedom". Her main aim is to heal people and make them smile through her art of writing. You can follow her on Instagram at dj_writes_to_heal.

Carved In The Pages Of My Soul

Your name is written on the pages of my soul,
Carved permanently capturing it whole.
You would soon be near, my heart I console;
Loving you endlessly is my motive and goal.

Carved your name in my heart forever,
Will pass this beautiful journey together.
Each moments we spent, I remember;
To explain it all I need love interpreter.

The ring on my finger I endlessly adore,
To visualize that beautiful day and restore.
With manuscripts my love hence I secure,
The spark is ever glowing just like before.

No love story is simple and sorted,
So has mine been a little distorted.
But assembling all the pieces scattered,
Loving you forever I hence move forward.

Yamini Sona Vaishnavi

Yamini Sona Vaishnavi is a budding writer who pursues her III UG of English Literature in Madurai, Tamil Nadu. She has a great love for playing with words and passion for reading and writing, especially poetry and quote writing. She is currently co-author for so many anthologies and wishes to write more. She started writing from her school days, where she used to contribute for yearly magazine and continued the same in her college too. She wishes to touch the hearts of the readers through her poetry.

When Confusions Felt Beautiful :

I think it was from my mom, in my age of five ...
I got the desire of a classical attire to get attached in my body!
It was an age where, I had a wish to get involved into my culture's representation!
A form of dance! A dance which is more than just expression! Equal to emotions!
And a form which represented the moves of lord!
It wasn't wrong that my mom wished me to get into it!
Neither my thought was proved wrong by anyone!
What hurt my deary mother was that after my practice I failed to perform,
Sort of circumstance felt very bad!
I felt bad as a child I failed to make my deary proud!
But opportunities are just like straight growing bamboo trees!
The height of the tree hit me once at my sixteen!
I performed as lead and transformed myself into a magnet that attracted mob!
I did it for an hour or so but all the while, every second I saw my mom smiling!
I saw the smiles all around! the cheers all around! the applause all around!
I heard appreciations that went straight into my ears and so did my diary!
I had people in my past who never felt I can do it!
I proved them not through words but through actions!
That a human being can only speak and find faults,
but an achiever may change the verdict of community!
Of course! I had been rejected several times! But what made my deary smile was,
the nature of being humble while I saw her smile carrying my award!
Of course! I was under so many confusions when I thought am I worthy enough!
When I never chose dance and it chose me in the right time in front of thousands,
I felt after days together that confusions at times can be so beautiful!

Sri Harsha Vineela Balla

Lady with a Child mindset...
Believes in flying the world....
Dream about finding love without pain...

What are good moments?
May be the ones that never makes us, to regret the things we have done and gives us a curve on our pretty faces.

But I think there are many in my life but there is one moment and the only moment where I could have given anything I owned in my life to stop the time. It has the power to make me feel the moment again and makes me sad and happy.

There is a saying" There is a thing that changes happy moment to sad and sad moment to happy. And the thing is TIME".

But the moment I am talking about is The night before my Big Day.

Yes, its crazy, sad, anxious ,happy, terrifying night in my life.

Every one will feel the same about their big day is what I learned after that.

Many things are happening right in front of my eyes. Everyone is busy till 2AM, shouting , dancing, playing.

But me in my room taking down my closet, folding the clothes alone. All my eyes could see is the Mehandi, which is making me leave MY HOME and tears started rolling down.

Its not the things that freaking me out but the later things that I should do…..

I will be away from everything that kept me happy and will be in search of new adventures of my life.

New Experirences with new people……

New traditions…..

New Relations…..

And all I know is No one will be there…..

I will be alone…..

My brother will be at home rolling on my bed with bag full of chips streaming shows…

My Dad will be in his business world earning for the bills….

My Mom will be in kitchen cooking for them…..

Nothing will be changed after today for them but for me everything changes…..

I wont be with my bro watching series…

I wont be there to increase the bill payments to my dad….

Christy Gnana Deepa. J

Christy Gnana Deepa , writer pursuing her Undergraduate in English literature in Madurai, Tamilnadu, India. She is a compiler of two anthologies, SECLUDED HEARTS and THE ARDENT HEARTS. Moreover, she is a co-author of more than 35 Anthologies. A writer by passion and a literarian by profession. You can follow her for more writeups in Instagram as ___budding___writer

Cherish Happy Moments

Everyday is a new beginning. Everyday brings us new hope and freedom. Everyday brings happy moments. Happy moments are to be cherished ever.

Happy moments, happy days, will not be forgotten because we love being happy and we cherish being happy.

Make each and every moment happy to feel the happy side of you.

Thus, my happy moment occurs whenever I come home from Hostel. It is a elated moment, because it is the the time to see my family, relatives and friends. That is the moment which I love the most.

Even if you don't have time to cherish happy moments, just feel the moment and make yourself happy.

Amritanshu Shreshth

Master Amritanshu Shreshth is a student of Open Minds A Birla School Kankarbagh, Patna, Bihar std. 9 with excellent academic performance and a distinguished skill in sports. With a magnificent start at the age of 12, he is an avid writer with a keen interest in life lessons and classical literature with some specific hobbies like playing guitar. He loves to express his feelings and life lessons with his write-ups. He had won many medals and certificates in Literature and Debates with his writing and speaking skills and had written many articles and science documentaries with his pen name Yuvraj.

Ablazed Ineffable Moments

Moments are the only thing that stays with someone regardless of the phase of life and helps in refreshing those beautiful times spend by them with their loved ones. Life is not a perfect one but it has perfect moments which we need to enjoy. The good moments are generally the one that you didn't plan buy yet it gave you happiness and helped in making your life a charming one. These moments are closest to one's heart and sometimes make one's heart. They are the only path your heart follows when you are surrounded by darkness. Remembering your happy moments are the only way to fill the ink of you life's pen and write a colourful life and continue making good moments.

As truly said, "Enjoy every single moment whether it be the good, the bad, the beautiful, the ugly, the inspiring, and the not so glamorous. Thanks God for it all". These moments can't be enjoyed again but can be remembered and felt whenever you want and give your life a new and cherishing start every day. Your hardest time often lead to the greatest moment of your life. So, rush through your adversities, make moments and achieve success with flying colours. Moments can be in any form just the fact being that we need to know that how to enjoy it. The world will be no more than heaven if you start enjoying each and every moments of your life.

So, let's cherish every moments into a good and ablaze memory by creating a mind-set to flourish every moment of this amazing life. The events of life are not repeatable but memories are the only thing you can feel and create to have a happy life. I like the most about a photograph is that it can capture moments that can never be reproduced again and are lost in the time like tears in the rain. Moments are created everywhere and every time just you need to carve it out of your life and make it a memory to remember. This world will end but moments will stay with you.

Shivani Batra

Shivani Batra is pursuing Msc in Biotechnology from Amity University, Noida. Her poetry is about the moments that we feel when we are with someone special and want to keep them with us forever and cherish those memories.

Kashtiyon ko lehro main doobta dekha tha maine,
Kinare main aake chahte hue bhi dekha tha maine,
Hawaon ka rukh aaj kuch alag sa tha,
Apno ko aaj barso baad muskurate dekha tha maine
Phulon se mehekte nanhe haath ,
Aangan main khelte vo nanhe pair
Waqt ne bhi aaj andaza lagaya hai,
Ye chaand maano peheli baar dekha tha maine,
Haathon main haath tumhara jaise jannat ki raahe ho,
Manzil ki fikar nahi khoobsoorat vo safar h jisme yaadein tumhari ho.

Kanchi Gupta

A simple girl in a big messy world trying to find her way through. She is currently building up the courage to process her ideas into words. She has faced the good and dark times just the like the ones before her and is now trying to make a difference by sharing her experiences to help others grow through it.

A New Start

And as the winds passed
it wouldn't end she thought.
The smiles had all passed away not to be seen for month,
Nay years.
As she picked herself up to push forth another day
She felt the touch of sun on her blistered skin,
Warming her the way she wished the hug of a lover would.
This little warmth powered her through the day and as the opportunities flooded by
she ran past them embracing them with a smile.
Today was a good day tomorrow will be better
The warmth will grow
This was just the beginning of the rest of the grass running charade
Talking to the birds and smelling the fresh wind was now her new hobby

The Realization

The wind in his hair
The sun across his face
Distant sound of children playing
Catch the ball they said
He finally drew himself out of his room to feel the fresh air
Now chasing the little boys across the field
Not even recognizing himself
The freshness in the air was a warm welcomed breath
Something he felt deeper within
It was laughter and joy
blissful euphoria
It was a bundle of his first kiss , his first touch !
And as he ran past there he saw her the new apple of his eye
Sheela was it or Humaira he couldnt decide
All he knew is that she would someday make a good wife
Asking her to join in the games his cards set right
Now for sure he was having the time of his life.

Keshav Tibrewal

Keshav Tibrewal is an accidental writer from Bhubaneswar, Odisha. He is a part time poet who creates something new only when he experiences something. His journey of writing was impossible without his mentors Anshuman Mohanty and Tejaswinee Nayak. Connect with him on Instagram- @_tibrewal.

Bada Acha Lagta Hai

Pyaar toh nahi hai tumse...
Magar tumhari aankho me khudko paana bada acha lagta hai,

Pyaar toh nahi hai tumse,
Magar tumhare mun se apna naam sunna bada acha lagta hai

Pyaar, toh nahi hai tumse,
Magar tumhara mujhe dekh kar muskurana bada acha lagta hai....

Pyaar toh nahi hai tumse,
Magar tumhara mujhe pyaar se jawab dena bada acha lagta hai......

Pyaar toh nahi hai tumse...
Magar meri darawni awaz ko acha bolna bada acha lagta hai...

Pyaar toh nahi hai tumse..
Magar tumhare message ka intezaar karna mujhe bada acha lagta hai....

Pyaar toh nahi hai tumse....
Magar tumare baare me sochna bada acha lagta hai....

Pyaar toh nahi hai tumse....
Magar tumhe jaanu kehe ke bulana bada acha lagta hai....

Pyaar toh nahi hai tumse....
Magar mai tumhara hun ye bolna bada acha lagta hai...

Pyaar toh nahi hai tumse....
Magar pyaar hai ye sochna bada acha lagta hai.....

Bhavika Dhiraj Sindhi

Bhavika Dhiraj Sindhi a 25-year-old
creative writer. She belongs to Turkey an Indian writing from abroad due to her passion in writing.
A BCom graduate.
She is writing since 7th std

A Stranger To My Forever

"In life, you don't need a lot. You need just one person to take a chance on you; one person, that's all it takes.
It could be a lover, a friend, a manager, a stranger, but whoever it is, has put on your shoulders an enormous debt. If you find someone like that, make sure you pay it back. At some point, when you come across someone who requires a teeny bit more effort, a chance, you better take it. They don't need a lot. They need you, at that moment, taking a chance on them. It's a cycle. It's how it all goes, and how it all has gone, and how it will always go. It's always been just strangers taking a chance on other strangers. it's the name of the game. We don't need a lot. We need strangers to trust others and we need the others to pay that debt back. That's how generations are made; Just a bunch of people taking countless leaps of faith every day; just a bunch of people going all in without looking at the cards. That's all we need. It's everything we've ever needed - strangers trusting strangers."

To the one stranger who came in my life...
All the time of my life I was struggling and was waiting for some magic until I found him and he gave me something so much more "It was REAL"
That's when I felt all my hardwork paid off...
I was happy to have him...
Whenever I felt good I ran to him
Wherever I felt bad I ran to him
Whenever I felt nothing I ran to him...
Because my mood swings were temporary and he is permanent and all mine...
You were the radiant sparkle to my life
Your smile is the best thing to make my day
Alll i love about is that I have you for lifetime and you gonna love me forever

Flairs and Glairs, a platform by a student for the students. We are esteemed youth struggling to carve out our path for our future and we follow a basic mindset Since everyone is not born with all-round skills. Joining hands with people who are born to execute it with perfection is the best way to evolve. Self-Evolution is the need of the hour but, evolving as a community is what we strive for. The initiative as kickstarted by, Founder- Mr. Shubham Shah with the motive to utilize the skillset and talent of writing has now a team of 10+ people who are actively participating into newer forms of learning and discovering talents among youngsters. We Provide platform and services like Publishing opportunities, Open mics, Workshops, Hands-on training. Operating with Brand Name of Flairs and Glairs (Publication House), we offer the chance of elevating a passionate writer to an esteemed author With Brand name Teekhe Zasbaaat. We bring to you an opportunity to get accustomed with the Public Speaking and Presenting of Thoughts along with regular challenges to brush up your inking spirit. The newest initiative to extend our services we introduced in a new writing Platform- The Glittering Fables and Ink Over Tears.

We Choose to Fly Like A Falcon than to be a Leg Pulling Crab.

To Know More: Infoline – 7781900870
Mail Us At-
flairsandglairs@gmail.com / info@flairsandglairs.in
Or Visit is at
www.flairsandglairs.com / www.flairsandglairs.in
Social Handles- @flairsandglairs @teekhezasbaaat

www.ingramcontent.com/pod-product-compliance
Ingram Content Group UK Ltd.
Pitfield, Milton Keynes, MK11 3LW, UK
UKHW022004190726
13853UKWH00004B/1719